Fearless Freddie

by Shelley Swanson Sateren

illustrated by Deborah Melmon

TABLE OF CONTENTS

ADVENTURES AT HOUND HOTEL

IT'S TIME FOR YOUR ADVENTURE AT HOUND HOTEL!

At Hound Hotel, dogs are given the royal treatment. We are a top-notch boarding kennel. When your dog stays with us, we will follow your feeding schedule, give them walks, and tuck them in at night.

We are always just a short walk away from the dogs — the kennels are located in a heated building at the end of our driveway. Every dog has his or her own pen, with a bed, blanket, and water dish.

Rest assured . . . a stay at the Hound Hotel is like a vacation for your dog. We have a large play yard, plenty of toys, and pool time in the summer. Your dog will love playing with the other guests.

HOUND HOTEL
WHO'S WHO

WINIFRED WOLFE

Hound Hotel is run by Winifred Wolfe, a lifelong dog lover. Winifred loves dogs of all sorts. She wants to spend time with every breed. When she's not taking care of the canines, she writes books about — you guessed it — dogs.

ALFIE AND ALFREEDA WOLFE

Winifred's young twins help out as much as they can. Whether your dog needs gentle attention or extra playtime, Alfreeda and Alfie provide special services you can't find anywhere else. Your dog will never get bored with these two on the job.

WOLFGANG WOLFE

Winifred's husband pitches in at the hotel whenever he can, but he spends much of his time traveling to study wolf packs. Wolfgang is a real wolf lover — he even named his children after pack leaders, the alpha wolves. Every wolf pack has two alpha wolves: a male one and a female one, just like the Wolfe family twins.

Next time your family goes on vacation, bring your dog to Hound Hotel.

Your pooch is sure to have a howling good time!

CHAPTER 1
Howling Like Mad

I'm Alfie Wolfe, and I'm here to tell you all about a fraidycat dog named Freddie.

Don't think I'm making fun of him. I know what it's like to be scared of stuff. Especially sharks. Man, sharks creep me out!

But this story isn't about killer fish. It's about Freddie. Freddie the beagle. Freddie with the howl like you wouldn't believe.

He checked into our dog hotel last June. I'll never forget that stormy week. We're talking huge, dark thunder clouds. Those clouds were the color of stormy ocean water full of seaweed. And sharks.

Back to Freddie. He showed up on a Saturday. The weather guy on TV had forecasted blue skies and tons of sunshine that weekend. Man, did he get it wrong.

That morning, a huge boom of thunder woke me partway up. I was lying inside my sleeping bag on our living room floor. I was at the tail end of a nightmare — still half asleep — and yelling stuff like, "Help! I'm inside a shark! It swallowed me whole!"

I kicked and punched and shoved, trying to bust my way out of that shark's stomach. A loud ripping sound, sort of like meat tearing off bones, made me stop and open my eyes.

I realized that I was at the bottom of my sleeping bag. All of me. My whole head and

body! Then I noticed that I'd torn a big hole in the bag down there.

I stuck my head out of the tear and looked around.

Our living room was as dark as the inside of a shark's stomach. It was noisy in there, too. I heard my own panting and rain pounding on the windows. I heard thunder rumbling outside and my sister laughing.

I looked over at her and saw that Alfreeda was inside her sleeping bag. But she was down at the very bottom of it, all curled up, laughing at me.

Her sleeping bag looked just like a shark that had swallowed a kid whole.

"Ha!" she cried. "You're afraid of sharks now *too*? Since when? We don't live anywhere near an ocean! Ha-ha-ha!"

Suddenly a super-loud boom of thunder shut her right up.

I thought, *Weird. Alfreeda never shuts up. And since when* HAVE *I been scared of sharks?* Then I remembered — they started freaking me out just the night before.

My family had been watching another dog movie. Well, my dad hadn't been watching. He was Up North, studying wolves in the wilderness. Just my mom, sister, and I watched it, cozy in our sleeping bags on the floor.

Somewhere in the middle of the movie, Mom had moved to the couch and fallen asleep. The second the movie ended, Alfreeda started to snore like a pug.

I'd gotten up to turn off the TV but sat right back down. A shark movie had come on, and I was interested. It was about a killer great white shark. The huge shark had terrified everyone in a beach town.

Before I even realized it, I'd watched the whole thing.

After that, it took me forever to fall asleep. I just kept chewing on my fingernails, like a dog with a tasty bone. Or like a shark chewing on someone's tasty leg.

I must've finally nodded off, though, because

there I was, waking up the next morning. Super-bright flashes of lightning turned the living room all white — as white as a great white shark's underside.

Loud claps of thunder made our windows shake. My sister was still curled up at the bottom of her sleeping bag. The bumpy lump of knees and elbows shook all over.

I couldn't believe she was laughing that hard at me, so hard that no noise came out. When somebody laughs that hard, the only thing that comes out is tears from the eyeballs.

It's not like I could laugh at her and call her a fraidycat. See, my sister is fearless. I hate that! She's not even scared of Spot, our rooster.

It's not like I'm scared of *all* roosters. But Spot charges us like a bull when he's bored. It's creepy. Alfreeda always laughs. I scream.

It's not fair that she's Alpha Kid in the Bravery Department around here. I figure that's because she was born five minutes before me. *Yeesh!*

Suddenly I heard Mom say, "Good morning, sleepyheads. Are you two up?" Her voice crackled over the walkie-talkie.

Alfreeda leaped out of her sleeping bag. She tore across the room and grabbed the walkie-talkie off the charger.

She pressed the *Talk* button and shouted, "Mom! Mom! Hi! Hi! Over! Over!"

"Why on earth are you shouting, Alfreeda?" Mom asked in that crackling voice. "And why are you repeating yourself? Never mind. I need you two down at the kennels on the double. The thunder is scaring Freddie, the little beagle," Mom's voice crackled on. "He's howling like mad and making the other dogs bark. I need one of you to calm him down, the other to do chores. Please hurry! Don't forget to brush your teeth. Over."

"Be right there, Mom!" Alfreeda shouted. "I'll handle Freddie. I'll calm him right down. Alfie will do *all* of the chores. Over! Over!"

"No way!" I yelled. "*I* get Freddie! Give me the walkie. Let me talk to Mom!"

Alfreeda laughed and tore up the stairs holding the walkie-talkie.

CHAPTER 2
A Scream that Breaks Glass

I tried to jump up and run right after my sister. But I got all tangled up in my sleeping bag. Finally I ripped my way out and tore up the stairs.

Alfreeda was in her dumb bedroom. I stepped in and shook my head at all her stuffed dogs. There must have been at least a hundred. Maybe two.

"Good luck finding the walkie," she said and grinned. "It's behind one of my dogs. Have fun doing chores while I play with Freddie."

"Wrong!" I yelled.

"Game on," she said and grinned. Then she dashed to the bathroom.

"You're *not* going to get to Freddie first!" I yelled. I dashed to my room to get dressed.

I dug through a bunch of piles on my floor. I looked everywhere for my jeans.

Then I saw them. They were on my legs. Just like that, I remembered — I'd slept in my jeans and a Hound Hotel T-shirt.

Ha! I was way ahead of my sister! I was totally ready to have a blast with my new bud Freddie. Then I remembered — Mom said to brush my teeth.

I tore to the bathroom.

My sister was already at the sink, brushing her teeth. She was all dressed for kennel work, too. Same as every day — blue jeans and a Hound Hotel T-shirt.

Then I remembered that she'd slept in her clothes, too. I groaned.

She spun around. "Why don't you knock?" she yelled. Her mouth was full of foamy toothpaste.

"The door was open!" I yelled back. "Stop yelling! You're spraying me with toothpaste!"

I wiped my cheeks and chin. Gross!

She spun back around and brushed faster.

Lightning-quick, I grabbed my toothbrush and gooped on toothpaste. The whole glob fell off the brush. It landed on the floor with a *splat*.

"You're cleaning that up," she said in her top-boss voice.

I frowned at her. My heart began to pound. Sea-foam covered her mouth. And her eyes had her normal morning look — dead-looking and beady-like. Like a certain kind of killer fish.

She spit the sea-foam into the sink and grabbed a glass to rinse. She rinsed and spit, then took a drink of water. Then she swallowed and turned to me. Her beady eyes stared right into mine.

"What are you *staring* at?" she demanded. She talked right into the empty glass.

Well, the bottom of the glass magnified her teeth. I'm telling you, they looked *huge*! And extra pointy! And super *sharp*!

I screamed — the kind of scream that's so loud it could break glass. That same second, three other things happened: thunder boomed and shook the house, Alfreeda screamed her head off, and she dropped the glass.

It shattered on the bathroom floor. It broke into hundreds of tiny pieces.

"You're cleaning that up," I said.

"Am not," she said.

"Are too," I said. "You dropped it."

"Well, you screamed and *made* me drop it," she said.

"You screamed too," I said.

"I screamed because *you* screamed," she said. "Why *else* would I scream?"

She had a point.

Alfreeda set her toothbrush tidy-like in our dog-shaped toothbrush holder. "See you out there, bro," she said. "Have fun doing chores." She leaped over the broken glass and landed in the doorway.

"No!" I shouted. "*I'm* playing with Freddie!"

— CHAPTER 3 —
Call Me Fraidycat

Alfreeda turned around. She leaned on the doorframe and sighed.

"Oh, Alfie," she said in her tired-teacher voice. "*Please* listen. Freddie doesn't want to *play* right now. He's *afraid*. He needs me to hug him. And cuddle him. He needs me to say, 'It's okay,' over and over. Get it?"

She had a point. Five points, to be exact.

"Besides," she said and rolled her eyes, "how could *you* make a scared dog feel better?"

Go ahead, I thought. *Call me fraidycat to my face. I dare you.*

"Don't cut yourself cleaning up," she said. "So long, bro!" She ran down the stairs. The back door slammed.

One second later, I heard a fierce clap of thunder and a shriek so loud it could've broken glass (if the glass hadn't already been broken).

The shriek came from outside. "Must have been a barn owl," I said to myself and headed for the broom.

Even though *I* didn't break it, I swept up the glass as fast as I could. I got only one little cut on my pinky finger.

That got me thinking about the cut a shark could make on someone's fingers. We're talking, goodbye *whole* hand!

Just thinking about it made me shake all

over. I got back to brushing my teeth, but I kept missing the toothbrush with the paste. A few more globs fell on the floor.

Finally, I got the brush covered. Then, faster than a shark can bite, I brushed my teeth. It only took about two seconds flat.

Don't think I'm bragging about my alpha-guy speed in toothbrushing. The trick is in the toothbrush. See, Mom buys a special kind for my sister and me. They're extra big so they clean more teeth extra fast.

Truth is, they're dog toothbrushes. That's really the only part of the store that our mom likes to shop in — the dog department. Sure, the brushes are shaped like chew bones. But they work great. I tossed my brush into the holder, spit, and ran downstairs.

Somehow, *I'd* get to play with good old Freddie *and* get out of doing stupid chores.

I dashed down our driveway to the kennel building. I got totally soaked in about two seconds flat. If I remember right, I think I dodged a few bolts of lightning too.

It was kind of fun. But not as much fun as I was going to have with Freddie! I threw open the front door of our dog hotel.

"Hey, Fred my man!" I yelled. "Get ready to party! Here comes Alfie!"

I don't think he heard me. A bunch of

howling and barking was coming from the kennels.

I dashed through the office, down the hall and into the big room at the back of the building. That's where the pens are. Or you can call them kennels. You can even call them runs if you want.

See, each run is big enough for a dog to run around inside. Get it?

I spotted Freddie right away, his nose anyhow. He was under his raised bed. (That's like a little kiddie bed, raised off the floor by short legs.) Freddie was hiding under his. He'd stopped howling now. The other dogs had gotten quiet, too.

Still, he was shivering like crazy and making quiet little crying sounds. Alfreeda was on her knees, wiggling her fingers at him.

"Come on out now, sweetie," she said in her talking-to-babies voice. "That horrible thunder is all over. You're okay, you're okay..."

He kept right on shivering.

"Oh, yeah, he looks *real* calmed down," I said to my sister.

She spun around and yelled, "Stop sneaking up on me like that!"

"I didn't sneak up on you!" I said.

"You did too!" she said and stared hard at me. Man, her eyes sure looked beady.

I froze, locked in a stare down, like a clown fish facing a great white shark. Finally, I tore my eyeballs away and pretended to read some information about Freddie.

Freddie's check-in form was on a clipboard that hung on the front of his pen door. Pretty soon, I got bored just standing there, so I actually started to read. This is what Freddie's owner had written:

Dear Hound Hotel workers,

Please beware when taking Freddie on walks . . . he's fearless. He'll chase after a wild pig. He'll charge a bull. Freddie only fears one thing — thunder. However, the weather report promises sunshine for the weekend. So all should be well.

I'm sure Freddie will have nothing but fun at your fine hotel. Thank you.

Yours truly,

Bob (Freddie's owner)

"What fun?" I said to myself. Freddie hadn't had a speck of fun yet!

Well, you can't be lazy when you run a dog hotel. I had to get cracking and help give good old Fred the best country vacation ever!

I marched right into his pen. He was still under his bed. Alfreeda was still begging him to come out, in that weird talking-to-babies voice.

"I'll handle this," I said. "Move over."

"No," she said.

"Mom!" I yelled.

CHAPTER 4
Seriously Not Funny

Mom came walking in from the laundry room. She carried a big basket of clean dog towels and blankets. She set the basket on a little table with wheels and wheeled the table to the middle of the room.

As she started to fold the laundry, she smiled at me. "Good morning, Alfie," she said.

"It's *not* a good morning," I said. "Alfreeda's hogging Freddie."

"Oh, you two silly dog lovers," Mom said.

"Always fighting over who gets to play with the cutest dogs. I can't blame you! But guess what, Alfie? I have some super-fun chores for you. A little Chihuahua just checked in. Would you please go to the storeroom and gather overnight things for him? Get an extra-small bed, a little blanket, a tiny water dish . . ."

"I don't see any Chihuahua," I said, looking around.

"He's in his outside run," Mom said. "In pen number four."

I looked at the doggie door at the back of that pen. See, every guest at our hotel has an outdoor run, too.

"What's his name?" I asked.

"Shark," Mom said.

I spun around and said, "That's *seriously* not funny, Mom."

"What's not funny?" she asked.

"Kidding me about his name," I said.

"Why would I kid you about something like that?" Mom said and handed me a towel. "Please dry him off when he comes inside. Oh look, there's Shark now."

Nice and slow, I turned around. I stared through the chain-link fence at the little itty-bitty dog. He stood as stiff as a shark fin, right in front of the doggie door he'd just plowed through. He dripped water all over the floor, like he'd just jumped out of the ocean.

"Go on, Alfie," Mom said. "Go into his pen and dry him off. Quickly, before he gets cold."

I held the towel tight against my stomach. I stepped toward Shark's pen. I stared at him. He stared at me. He took a step in my direction. He narrowed his eyes at me and growled.

Then he opened his mouth super wide! I saw tons of pointy, sharp-looking teeth. *Shark teeth!*

Right then, four things happened at exactly the same time: Shark sprang straight toward me, I screamed, a super-loud boom of thunder shook the building, and Alfreeda gave a terrible shriek.

I jumped back and knocked over the little table on wheels. Clean blankets and towels flew *everywhere!*

"Alfie!" Mom cried. "I just folded those!"

CHAPTER 5
Cut That Out!

Man, Freddie sure howled at that last boom of thunder. He closed his eyes and threw back his head with a "*Wah-oooohhh!*"

His howl made all five of the big dogs bark. Shark started in too. I kept seeing every big tooth inside that little dog's mouth.

At some point, Freddie had leaped onto Alfreeda's lap. That's where he was now, shaking and shivering. He shook so hard that he made my sister shake too.

Mom didn't say anything to anyone. She just calmly picked up the table. Then she picked up all the towels and blankets. Next, she headed into Shark's pen. She picked him up, dried him off with a towel, and kissed him on the head.

After she had Shark settled in his kennel, she put on some music. She turned the volume way up.

Ugh. The first song she played was my sister's favorite. The song was the stupidest pop song of all time. Part of it goes: "Oh baby, I'm lovin' our happy, sunshine-y, baby-blue-sky day."

I hate that song. Almost more than sharks. But Freddie stopped howling right away. The other dogs stopped barking. Maybe that song could brainwash dogs.

Alfreeda buried her face in the back of Freddie's neck. She rocked him back and forth and kept saying, "It's okay, it's okay."

Freddie started to shiver all over again.

Before the song even ended, Mom turned down the volume. *Thank. You. Mom.*

She started to fold the laundry again. "So, Alfie and Alfreeda," she said and smiled at us. "A minute ago, both of you screamed as if the world were ending. Want to talk about it?"

"Nope," Alfreeda and I said at the same time.

"Okay," said Mom with a smile.

At that second, more thunder rumbled. Lightning flashed. My sister buried her face in Freddie's neck again. Poor guy. What if her nose was running or something? Disgusting!

Man, Freddie was having zero fun. I had to get him unscared so we could play catch or something. Maybe I'd build him a storm-chaser van, and we'd pretend to zoom after twister clouds and stuff.

But I had to get him calmed down first! And I knew just how to do it.

"Hey, Freddie, old boy," I said. "I'll run the clothes dryer for you. The humming will calm you down, real quick. See, one time a stray cat jumped out of a tree and landed on our dad's back. Dad sat by the dryer for about an hour before he calmed down."

Alfreeda looked at me and smiled a little.

"Oh, yeah," she said. "I remember that. Dad's so creeped out by cats. Let's go, Freddie."

She picked him up and carried him to the laundry room. I followed.

"Wait, Alfie," Mom called. "What about chores?"

"But Freddie needs me," I called over my shoulder. "I'm the Alfie Male in this pack. It's my job to get the underdogs unscared!"

"All right," she said and laughed.

I dashed to the laundry room. Alfreeda already had the dryer running. It rattled and thumped.

She sat on the floor and leaned against the dryer. Freddie was in her lap. She kept saying, "It's okay."

But the thunder was getting even louder.

The rain was coming down harder, too. It hammered the window above the dryer.

I climbed on top of the dryer and looked outside. "Man!" I said. "The play yard's flooded! It's never rained this much."

"I know," Alfreeda said. Her voice came out kind of squeaky.

"You're talking weird," I said.

"Am not," she squeaked.

I shrugged and said, "Know what? If the play yard is flooded, that means the lake is too." The lake was right on the other side of a hill, not far from the play yard.

"And that means the rivers are flooded," I said. My voice was coming out squeaky now, too. "If the rivers are flooded, the oceans are. That means that sharks are swimming upriver from the ocean."

"I bet they're swimming from the river to the lake to the play yard," I squeaked on. "They're waiting out there for us, with their jaws wide open! When the sun comes out, we'll go outside to play, and sharks will turn us into their afternoon snack!"

My heart pounded like a hammerhead shark. I looked at my sister. Her eyes rolled so far back in her head that they turned almost totally white.

"Cut that out!" I cried.

She unrolled her eyeballs and sighed. "Alfie," she said in her tired-teacher voice. "You're not even making sense. We live hundreds of miles from an ocean. Sharks can't swim this far. Besides, they need salt water. Sharks don't like human meat anyhow. We're too bony."

"Really?" I squeaked.

"Yeah," she said. "A shark takes a bite out of someone's leg, says yuck, and spits it out."

"Then why do they bite people in the first place?" I demanded.

"Because they think you're a nice fat juicy seal," she said.

"Me?" I cried.

"Not you!" she said. "There aren't any sharks around here, Alfie! What's *wrong* with you?"

"Uh, I watched a shark movie last night," I said. I told her the name of the movie.

"You're kidding," she said and whistled. "Wow. Does Mom know?"

I shook my head.

"That's like the scariest movie of all time," Alfreeda said. "Well, trust me, Alf. There are *no* sharks near us, okay?"

I was trying my best to believe her when a super-loud clap of thunder went *BOOM*! Freddie bolted off Alfreeda's lap. He started to howl and tore out of the laundry room.

Alfreeda jumped up and dashed after him. "Freddie, come back, it's okay," she called. Her voice came out all whispery. And I know why, too . . .

Because she'd just screamed her head off! It's true! I'd seen it with my own eyeballs. I'd heard it with my own eardrums. She'd opened her big mouth even wider and screamed so loud that she'd lost her voice!

I couldn't believe it. My sister, Alpha Girl, was *scared of thunder*. She never used to be but — for some reason — she was now! *Ha!*

I leaped off the dryer and chased after her. I couldn't wait to laugh in her face.

CHAPTER 6
Sir Lightning Bolt

It turned out that I couldn't laugh in my sister's face. I couldn't even see her face.

I found Alfreeda and Freddie in the storeroom. A blanket covered Alfreeda's head and whole body. Freddie was under there with her. He was howling his head off.

I yanked the blanket off them. Freddie looked at me and stopped howling right away.

"Hey!" I said in a super-firm voice. "How come you're acting scared of thunder and lightning?"

"Don't yell at Freddie," she said. "He can't help it."

"Not him!" I said. "I'm talking to you! Look, *you* can't be scared of thunder and lightning — or anything! Someone's got to be the bravest in the pack around here. Remember that time a stray cat jumped on Mom's head in the chicken coop? She shrieked her head off." Both our parents are creeped out by cats!

"You're the only totally brave top dog around here!" I added in my firmest voice. "You *have* to act strong — so the underdogs around here will feel safer!"

"I c-c-can't," she whispered.

"But what happened?" I asked. "You never used to be creeped out by thunderstorms."

"I'll tell you what happened," she said. "Yesterday Mom and I took some dogs on a walk through the woods. We saw this really big tree, split in half, with burn marks on it. Lightning had hit it! But get this: a bunch of smaller pieces of wood had split off the tree and sprayed all over. They must've been flying super fast because they were stuck in other trees, just like arrows! If animals or people had been nearby . . . Oh, man." Alfreeda stopped talking and shivered.

"Wow," I said. "Cool! I've got to see that! Anyhow, you're safe in here. There aren't any windows. Lightning can't get in."

"I'm still totally spooked. I can still hear the thunder," she squeaked. "And maybe there's a crack in the wall. Lightning could get in and get my toes or something."

"Lightning can come through cracks?" I asked.

She nodded, sure of herself.

My sister was top fact collector around our place, too. So I just shrugged and said, "Oh."

Then I got an idea. "I know," I said. "We could build a lightning-safe wall. Thick and solid, like a castle. Let's do it!"

"No," Alfreeda said. She yanked the blanket over her head and Freddie's head, too.

"Fine," I said. "I'll build it myself."

"Hurry," said Alfreeda. "Freddie's got bad breath. I can't be under here forever."

"You got it," I said. Then, at alpha-guy speed, I built a tall castle wall, right in front of the two fraidycats.

First, I found a bunch of big boxes. They were full of dog treats and toys and stuff. Nothing too heavy.

Next, I made a row of five boxes across.

Then I stacked four more rows on top of that one. I stood on a chair to build the top row.

"The rampart's done," I said.

"The what?" asked Alfreeda.

"The rampart — the wall," I said. "Now I'll build the battlement."

"The what?" she asked.

"You'll see," I said, grabbing some small boxes. I set them in a row on top of the rampart, except I left a large space between each one.

"Done with the battlement," I said. "See? You can look between the boxes. You can see right away if the bad guy is coming. If you see Sir Lightning Bolt blasting straight at you, get your bow and arrow ready.

"If you see his ghost-white knights and his

ghost-white war horses coming, too, get a
bunch of bows and arrows ready," I added.
"Make sure Freddie has one."

"I can't see over the top," she said. "I'm
standing on my toes even. The wall's too high."

"Oh," I said. "Well, don't you feel safer? How about Freddie? He's better, right? I totally boxed you in."

"A box has four sides," she said.

"So I *triangled* you in," I said. "Whatever."

"Why are there teeny cracks between all the big boxes?" she asked.

"They're arrow slits," I said.

"Alfie," she said in that same old tired-teacher voice. "Freddie and I don't have arrows. Or bows. Besides, lightning would burn them right up. And there's no drawbridge. How are we supposed to get out of here?"

"Be right back," I said and ran to the office.

I dug in the desk drawer and found a marker. I dashed back to the storeroom and drew some lines on the big boxes, super quick.

"There," I said. "I drawed a bridge."

"You *drew* a bridge," Alfreeda corrected me.

"I drew a drawbridge," I said. "Whatever."

She started to shout, "A drawn drawbridge doesn't do us any good! Get us *out* of here!"

She must've started to kick the boxes because they all tumbled down, right on top of my head. I shoved the boxes off, then rubbed my head and arms and shoulders. Nothing hurt too much.

I stared at my weird sister. Her hands were on her hips. She frowned at me.

"What?" I asked.

Just then, loud thunder rumbled outside. Alfreeda started to shiver all over again.

"Look," she said in a shaky voice, "I gave *you* the shark facts. You need to give me the *lightning* facts! Tell me there aren't any cracks in these walls! Tell me that lightning can't come through cracks anyhow! Tell me that, yeah, lightning can maybe come through an open window, but we don't have any windows open!

She kept on squeaking. "And tell me that thunder's nothing to be scared of, because when you hear it, lightning has already struck somewhere else! Tell me that thunder can't hurt you! You need to be *firm* about the facts, Alfie!"

"You just were," I said.

"But I don't believe me," she squeaked. "Maybe I'd believe *you*."

"That doesn't even make sense," I said. "Just snap out of it. What about Freddie, huh? He hasn't had any fun with you in charge. Come on, Freddie. Let's go hang out."

I clapped and whistled. "Let's go, bud," I said. "Let's play catch in the office." I grabbed a ball off a shelf.

He didn't move. Then I realized that he couldn't. He was all wrapped up in that blanket.

"What'd you do?" I asked my sister. "Wrap the blanket around him ten times or what?"

"Seven," she said.

"Well, unwrap him," I said. "He's not a hot dog."

"No," she said. "It makes him feel safer."

"Does not," I said. "Look, he's still shivering."

Even louder thunder rumbled outside. "Alfie?" my sister squeaked. "Would you please go get my sleeping bag?"

"Why should I?" I asked.

"If I feel safer, then I can make Freddie feel safer," she said. "I'll give you fifty cents."

"A dollar," I said.

"Deal," she agreed.

I kicked boxes out of the way and headed for the door.

"Alf?" she squeaked.

"What?" I said over my shoulder.

"You're going outside, in the middle of this terrible thunderstorm, for *me?*" she squeaked.

"No!" I said. "For Freddie!"

"Well," Alfreeda said, "when it comes to bravery, you're the Al—"

"No time to talk," I interrupted her. "I'll get my sleeping bag, too. And some pillows, and leftover popcorn from last night. We'll have a sleepover in Freddie's pen. Then he won't have to sleep all by his fraidycat self tonight. *Finally* some fun. Be right back."

I bolted outside, into the pouring rain, and leaped over every puddle. Just in case some baby sharks had swum upriver by mistake.

— CHAPTER 7 —
I'm a Goner!

Pretty soon, the three of us were back in Freddie's pen.

Alfreeda and Freddie were inside her sleeping bag. She looked like shark lunch, all curled up at the bottom.

Freddie sat in the middle. Every time he howled at loud thunder, he threw back his head. The howling bump looked just like a shark's fin.

"This is boring," I said.

Nobody heard me. Mom was playing some pop music really loud and singing along. She was brushing a big poodle too. She kept dancing around the poodle, brushing to the beat of the music.

The big dogs watched her. The thunder wasn't making them shiver or anything. Nope. Mom and the big dogs were totally acting like it was a sunshine-y, baby-blue-sky day.

I looked at Shark. He was sitting in the pen next door and staring at Alfreeda's shivering lump. He shivered, too.

"Hey, Shark," I said. "Stop watching my sister."

He looked at me.

"You know," I told him, "a guy can catch a bad case of fear, just like a bad cold. If you hang around a fraidycat, you can catch it.

Even if you're a dog. See the big guys who are watching my mom? They're calm as anything."

Shark looked back at Alfreeda. He started to shiver again. I got up and marched into his pen. I picked him up, marched out, and headed to the office.

About halfway there, I realized that Shark's teeth were about two inches from my neck. My heart started to pound. *I'm a goner!* I thought. *I'm shark meat! Goodbye sweet life!*

But I stopped and said to myself in a firm voice, "I'm fine." And surprise, I was!

I headed to the office desk and pulled open the top drawer. Setting Shark inside, I said, "Dig away, little dude. I'm looking for a deck of cards. I know it's here somewhere. Help me find it, okay?"

Well, that teensy Chihuahua started to dig

like a terrier. But he was zero help in finding those fifty-two cards.

He kept bumping his nose against Mom's goofy old mask. It had a fake nose, fake glasses, and a fake mustache. Back when my sister and I were little, we'd get scared of big dogs sometimes. Mom would put on that mask and make us laugh. We'd totally forget about being afraid.

Shark bumped it again with his nose. "Want to try it on?" I asked.

He yipped, which I figured meant yes. I put the mask on him. It was way too huge for his puny head.

"Wear it as long as you like, pal," I said. "We could use some laughs around this place today."

Then I dug some more and found the deck of cards.

"Okay, Shark, my man," I said, "here's the plan. First, we'll unscare my sister. Then Freddie. It has to be in that order, see, because Freddie thinks Alfreeda is his pack leader. Got it?"

Shark looked at me through the goofy mask.

I laughed, and we headed back to Freddie's pen.

CHAPTER 8
Woo-hoo, Won Again

A few seconds later, I poked Alfreeda's knee. Or maybe it was her elbow.

"Hey," I said. "Want to play War?"

"No," she said.

I couldn't believe my eardrums! War was my sister's all-time favorite card game. I hated it because she always won. How she could win a game of chance every time, I don't know.

"You can shuffle," I said.

"We don't have to flip a coin?" she asked.

"Nope," I said. "I'm letting you shuffle first. Come on."

"Okay," she said and squeezed past Freddie. She crawled right out and grabbed the cards from me.

Then she saw Shark and laughed. The laugh was weak, but still.

We sat on top of my ripped-up sleeping bag. Alfreeda started to shuffle.

"You can watch," I said to Shark. He sat between us.

Suddenly a big boom of thunder made Alfreeda jump about a foot. She screamed and threw all the cards in the air.

I didn't even lose my cool. "Hey," I said. "It's raining cards. No problem. I'll pick them up."

Alfreeda looked sideways at me. "You're acting weird, Alfie Wolfe," she said.

For once in my life I didn't say, "You're acting weirder, Alfreeda Wolfe." I just crawled all over Freddie's pen, lightning-quick, and picked up all the cards.

That put Alfreeda in a good mood. Beating me at War three times in a row put her in a *great* mood. She kept yelling, "I declare war!" and winning every time.

After the second game, I hauled Freddie out of Alfreeda's sleeping bag. I held him on my lap. He kept looking back and forth between Shark and my sister.

She and I started a fourth game. She yelled, "I declare war!" for about the hundredth time.

With no warning, a huge boom of thunder rattled the windows.

Alfreeda collected her cards and went, "Woo-hoo, won again."

I tapped her arm. "Guess what?" I said.

"What?" she asked.

"It just thundered super loud," I said.

"No it didn't," she said.

"Did too," I said. "You didn't jump or scream."

"Really?" she asked. "Wow. And hey, Freddie's not howling!"

"That's because he's watching you," I said. "I figured it all out."

"Figured what out?" she asked.

"See, dogs look to their leader, right?" I said. "Well, dogs don't understand what thunder is. They look to their leader to figure out how to feel. If you act like nothing's wrong, he'll feel brave too."

Alfreeda stared at me for about a minute. Then she said, "Know what, Alf? That actually makes sense."

"Naturally," I said. "Hey, want to play storm chasers with the dogs? We could use that little table on wheels and build a storm-chaser van. Freddie and Shark could ride inside. We could pretend to chase all kinds of bad weather! We could make storm movies for the weather channel!"

"Yeah!" she said. "We could make a dashboard, with a computer on it."

"And a radio dish for the top of the van," I said.

"Cool," she said. "I'll go get the marker and an empty box."

"Grab the table, too, okay?" I said. "Us guys will play catch in the office until you get there. Come on, Fred and Shark Man. Race you!"

The three of us raced to the office. Freddie won.

I pushed furniture out of the way, then threw the ball to Freddie. He caught it in his mouth, first try!

Then Shark and I chased him around, trying to get the ball back. We couldn't catch him.

Well, Freddie was just doing what beagles do best — tearing around and around and never getting tired!

"We're finally having some fun!" I said.

Freddie grinned at me and dropped the ball. I'm. Not. Kidding.

Good old Fred *grinned*.

Is a Beagle the Dog for You?

Hi! It's me, Alfreeda!

I bet you want your own cute, adorable beagle now too, right? Of course you do! Beagles LOVE kids and make great pets for families! But before you zoom off to buy or adopt one, here are some important facts you should know:

Beagles are super active! They'll play for hours . . . then want to keep on playing! They love to run around outside and play all kinds of games. So if you're the kind of family that likes to stay inside and watch TV a lot, DON'T get a beagle (or any dog). Get a pet rock.

Beagles LOVE to eat, and they eat a LOT. Some can eat more than bigger dogs. On walks, they'll try to eat any old thing that's on the ground. Beagles have a super-strong sense of smell and can find food that's hidden away, too. They'll get overweight fast if they don't get enough exercise. If you can't promise to play with your beagle and walk with her every day, do NOT get one. Paint your pet rock to look like a beagle.

Beagles follow their powerful smelling noses everywhere! They'll tear down the street or into the woods, smelling one curious smell after another. It's easy for a beagle to get lost. They HAVE to be on leashes or in a fenced-in yard to stay safe outside.

Okay, signing off for now . . . until the next adventure at Hound Hotel!

Yours very factually,

Alfreeda Wolfe

VISIT
HOUND HOTEL
AGAIN WITH
THESE AWESOME
ADVENTURES!

Learn more about the people and pups of Hound Hotel
www.capstonekids.com

ADVENTURES AT HOUND HOTEL

Homesick Herbie

WRITTEN BY
Shelley Swanson Sateren

ILLUSTRATION BY
Deborah Melmon

ADVENTURES AT HOUND HOTEL

Growling Gracie

...ren

ILLUSTRATION BY
Deborah Melmon

ADVENTURES AT HOUND HOTEL

Mudball Molly

WRITTEN BY
Shelley Swanson Sateren

ILLUSTRATION BY
Deborah Melmon

About the Author

Shelley Swanson Sateren grew up with five pet dogs — a beagle, a terrier mix, a terrier-poodle mix, a Weimaraner, and a German shorthaired pointer. As an adult, she adopted a lively West Highland white terrier named Max. Besides having written many children's books, Shelley has worked as a children's book editor and in a children's bookstore. She lives in Saint Paul, Minnesota, with her husband, and has two grown sons.

About the Illustrator

Deborah Melmon has worked as an illustrator for over 25 years. After graduating from Academy of Art University in San Francisco, she started her career illustrating covers for the *Palo Alto Weekly* newspaper. Since then, she has produced artwork for over twenty children's books. Her artwork can also be found on giftwrap, greeting cards, and fabric. Deborah lives in Menlo Park, California, and shares her studio with an energetic Airedale Terrier named Mack.